RAISING THE MOON

B.T. SINCLAIR

ISBN-13: 9781234567890

ISBN-10: 1477123456

Print ISBN: 979-8-9875101-3-1

Cover design by: Marta at Get Covers

Library of Congress Control Number: 2018675309

Printed in the United States of America

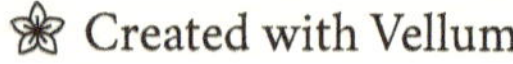 Created with Vellum

To Chris and Thea, with all my love -

PROLOGUE

The Fae are beautiful, ethereal beings with an immense kindness, and a love for music and dance. They prefer to dwell in secluded places such as forests, meadows, and streams, and are notoriously difficult to capture or interact with.

The Fae of the Hemlock Wilds raise and lower the moon - which is a crucial task in maintaining the balance of nature. All Fae in the world have different tasks, such as maintaining the seasons or ensuring the fertility of the land.

Despite their playful and mischievous nature, Fae can also be dangerous to humans who disrespect their territory or refuse to honour their customs and traditions...

* * *

As a blue wood Aster fae, Ardere was a master of camouflage and concealment - able to blend seamlessly into the natural surroundings of the forest. She spent her days carefully planted near a Noble Fir tree closest to the local mortal village of Thornbrook, keeping a watchful eye out for any mortals who might wander too close to the Fae realm.

Ardere took her duties zealously, knowing that the safety of her fellow Fae depended on her vigilance. She would often spend hours at a time scanning the horizon, watching for any signs of danger. If a mortal was spotted approaching, Ardere would sound the alarm by releasing some of her petals, and the cerulean folioles would waft back to the central lake further in their forest that the fae set up their homes. As long as Ardere was on duty, the Hemlock Wilds remained a sanctuary for all who dwelled within its boundaries.

* * *

Calida looked around, disoriented and confused. She did not know where she was or how she got there. Looking down, it surprised her to see her tawny webbed feet lightly treading cool, blue water.

As she took in her surroundings, she noticed a group of animals gathered around her, looking at her with curious eyes.

"Who am I?" Calida asked a chocolatey-colored rabbit close to the edge of the lake.

"You are Fae," replied the rabbit. "You were born

from the sacrifice of Ardere, a faerie who was killed by greedy mortals. I am Nettelia. We are all your family now," the gentle Fae informed Calida kindly.

Calida nodded to Nettelia, but paused after ruminating on the tragic news of her existence. She looked at her new sisters in shock and horror. They knew all too well the dangers posed by humans who carelessly destroyed the natural world around them.

"We must protect our way of life," Calida spoke softly but firmly. "We must protect our kind at all costs."

"We will protect our land," a petite Fae with coal black skin and matching silky hair declared. "The Hemlock Wilds represent something greater than ourselves. We vow to never let our home into the hands of the greedy mortals who had caused the death of Ardere," she finished resolutely.

CALIDA

I wake up early in the morning, eager to start my day. Heading out to the extensive garden and taking a deep breath, relishing in the scent of the freshly turned soil. I tend to the plants, and I feel a connection to the earth that is hard to describe. I water a nearby strawberry patch and check on my vegetables, all the while feeling a sense of satisfaction with each task completed. As the hours pass, I lose track of time and become lost in the beauty of my surroundings. I watch as butterflies and bees flit from flower to flower, and I feel a sense of pride in the role that I play in sustaining their habitats.

As the sun sets and the day draws to a close, I take one last look around my garden before heading back to my home. I feel a sense of accomplishment knowing that I have done my part in creating something beautiful and sustainable. I see my small, moss-covered cottage nestled amongst the trees, and I smile.

The thick layer of soft, green moss gives my little home a magical feel. The thatched roof is a patchwork of earthy browns and greens, with small vines growing up the sides. A small chimney puffs gentle plumes of smoke, showing that the fireplace inside is likely lit.

The windows are small and framed with simple wooden shutters. Small flower boxes filled with blue wood aster adorn the windowsills, spilling over with vibrant cerulean blooms. I planted them to feel close to the mother I never got to meet - I tend to these flowers with loving care, ensuring that they receive just the right amount of sunlight and water.

As I let myself in through the front door, which is painted a cheery but pale shade of yellow and adorned with a small brass knocker in the shape of a fox, I am greeted by the warm glow of a fire and the sweet scent of the bread that had finally finished rising. My interior is simple but cosy, with a small kitchenette where the walls are lined with shelves filled with jars of home-made jams and preserves, and a small table in the centre of the room holds a vase of wildflowers.

I look over at my living area with its comfortable woollen armchair and a bookshelf filled with well-loved tomes nestled next to the wood-burning fire-place, and I smile at my humble abode.

In the far corner of the room, I eyed longingly at my cosy twin bed, covered in a soft quilt made from patches of different fabrics spun on my loom. It is a haven of peace and comfort, a place where one can truly feel at home amid nature's beauty.

But there is no time to rest, as my sisters are already busy at work preparing for the sun to be replaced by its nighttime counterpart. I take a cloth and wipe the grime from the day off of my face, and assess myself in the mirror. Powder-blue eyes looked over my pale skin that had been lightly caressed by the noon sun. I grab a brush and drag it through my thick yellow hair until it is silky again. I am tall, almost six feet tall, and I have to step back from the mirror to gauge the cleanliness of my outfit. The dirt and sweat from the day seems to have seeped into my coveralls, and I quickly grab a flowy blue dress and change into that instead. With one last look around my home, I make my way out of my home and close the door softly behind me.

I feel a sense of anticipation building within me. The path is familiar, winding through the forest, leading me to the secluded lagoon surrounded by willow trees. As I walk, the sounds of nature fill my ears. Birds sing sweetly in the trees, crickets chirp in the grass, and the gentle rustling of leaves in the breeze creates a soothing melody. The path becomes more rugged and uneven as I make my way closer to the lagoon.

Finally, I arrive at the clearing where the lagoon sits, and I am met with a familiar but breathtaking sight. The water is crystal clear and shimmers as the sun sets. The branches of the willows hang low over the water, creating a canopy that filters the sunlight into dappled patterns on the surface of the water. I see my sisters busy working, plucking stars from the surrounding meadow and collecting them in large, handwoven wicker baskets.

A night sky takes hard work and technique. My family collects the stars each sunset to be cast into the sky once the sun sets. In the morning, as the sun rises once again, the stars are pushed back to earth to be planted and plucked again and again. But I have been entrusted with the responsibility of raising the moon itself. Once the sky is enveloped in stars, I walk to a hollow redwood tree past the willows and carefully grab the silvery orb. It is palm sized now, but when I usher the moon into its starting place, the size will multiply a million-fold.

I notice the stars have been properly scattered, each twinkling and shimmering with its own unique radiance. The stars seem to dance and twirl in the dark expanse, creating a mesmerising display that fills me with a sense of peace and tranquillity. The longer I look, the more stars I see, each one beckoning me to explore the mysteries of the universe. It's a beautiful reminder of the vastness and complexity of the world I live in, and a humbling experience that leaves me feeling small but connected to something infinitely larger than myself.

I shake my head, clearing it. As I stand here on the edge of the lake, I feel a strange energy coursing through my body. It starts with a tingling sensation in my fingertips, then spreads throughout my limbs, enveloping me in a warm glow. My muscles tense, and I feel a sudden rush of adrenaline as my body changes. My arms stretch and elongate, my fingers fusing together into a long, slender wing. White feathers sprout from my skin, first in small patches, then spreading rapidly until they cover my entire body. I can feel my bones shifting, growing lighter and more flexible, adapting to my new form. As the transformation ends, I feel a sudden urge to move, to take flight. I spread my wings wide, feeling the cool air rush through my feathers. I leap into the air, and the world drops away beneath me. As I circle above the lake, I look down at my reflection and see a beautiful swan staring back at me. I am filled with a sense of gratitude for this gift and a newfound appreciation for the beauty and grace of nature.

I bring the moon to its nightly station, and flutter back towards the earth. I transform back into my human form, and a few sisters congratulate me for another success in raising the moon.

ERISSA

The village of Thornbrook is a quaint, small town nestled in the rolling hills of the countryside. The sun rises early over the surrounding fields, casting a warm glow over the landscape. Erissa wakes up in her small room in her foster family's cottage, feeling groggy but content after a restful night's sleep. She stretches and rubs the sleep from her eyes before getting dressed for the day ahead.

After serving breakfast for her family, Erissa sets out to explore the village. She enjoys walking through the cobblestone streets, admiring the quaint shops and cottages along the way. She stops by the local bakery to pick up a sweet pastry, enjoying the smell of fresh bread and pastries as she browses the selection. As per usual, the townspeople are quick to dismiss her. For as long as Erissa can remember, the members of Thornbrook treated Erissa with unveiled disgust. The adults were unwelcoming, and would not let the other children play with her - and Erissa's days were lonely. All the pestering in the world would not convince Erissa's parents to explain the strange way everyone behaved towards her.

She does not tell her family this, but Erissa has started exploring closer and closer to the Hemlock Wilds. They fascinate her, and although it would be met with resounding disapproval, she cannot seem to help herself. The sunlight filters through the canopy of trees, creating patterns of light and shadow on the forest floor. The warmth of the sun feels comforting and relaxing, and the fresh, earthy smell of the woods fills Erissa's senses.

As she walks deeper into the woods, she notices the different shades of green that make up the foliage. The leaves of the trees are a vibrant green, while the ferns and moss on the forest floor are a softer, muted green.

She can't help but feel a sense of peace and serenity as the natural beauty is taken in. The soft crunch of leaves and twigs underfoot, and the occasional snap of a twig as an animal scurries by, are the only sounds that break the stillness of the woods. On the base of a Noble Fir tree further ahead, a sign warns: "Here Be Faeries." Erissa had never gone past the sign - no human that passed this boundary had returned alive. Nevertheless, it was as if an invisible force was pushing her onward.

Unconsciously, Erissa reached a hand out towards the dark grey bark. A small twig snapping dragged her back to reality, and Erissa flinched. Time had passed more quickly than she realised and her parents would wonder where she was, and where their supper was. She picked up the pace and was thankful that their humble home rested on the edge of their town. She breathed a sigh of relief when she saw her parents had not arrived yet. Grabbing a cast-iron skillet, she prepared the salmon. Her parents walked through the door as the meal was almost done cooking and they sat at the worn wooden table, ready to be served.

"Those blasted fiends," her father roared at no one in particular.

Erissa sighed quietly, knowing there was no escape from tonight's rant.

"I know dear, I know," Erissa's mother put a comforting hand on top of his.

"They have magic, and they hoard it for themselves! Those worthless Fae are undeserving of everything they have." Erissa's father's face had turned red, and he was panting.

Erissa had heard her father's rantings time and time again. Everyone knows that Fae have special gifts, talents, even. But while most believed these were gifts Fae are born with, Erissa's father is one of the vocal few that believed the Fae have learned these powers and greedily kept them for themselves. Erissa was not convinced, but kept her opinions to herself.

Her parents excused themselves from the dinner table, leaving Erissa to clean up after them. She could hear them still discussing their animosity towards the Fae, and she knows she will get time to herself tonight.

The Hemlock Wilds are calling to her, and she knows that this time she will answer.

Donning a lightweight green cloak, Erissa used the cover of darkness to make her way back to the fir tree. Without hesitation, she passes it and walks deeper through the woods. Erissa passes a lake surrounded by cottages and knows she is on the right track. Coming upon a meadow filled with stars, she quietly gasps. Entranced, Erissa watches the ethereal fae launch them into the sky.

The fae move with a graceful fluidity, and their delicate hands seem to possess an otherworldly power. Erissa can't help but marvel at the spectacle before her. The sky is dark and infinite, and yet the Fae seem to navigate it with ease. With each flick of their fingers, a new star bursts into being, illuminating the darkness and filling Erissa's heart with a sense of hope and possibility.

Erissa hesitates for a moment, unsure of her next step. Just as she is about to leave her hiding place, she notices a beautiful blonde woman walking purposefully towards a redwood tree, and reaching deep inside. Erissa is astonished as the woman pulls out a small, glowing silver orb. Placing the orb at her feet, the woman transforms into a magnificent swan. The swan plucks the orb with her webbed feet and takes flight, and Erissa watches in silent awe as the moon itself is cast into the night sky.

ERISSA

The walk back to her home seems to drag on, and Erissa tries to reflect on her thoughts and connect with the natural world. Walking in silence allows her to focus on her breathing and the sound of her footsteps, but it is not enough. As she takes in her surroundings, she notices details of the Hemlock Wilds, such as the way the light filters through the trees and the sounds of birdsong.

Were my parents right? Erissa wondered to herself, as she passed the Noble Fir.

Are the Fae harnessing the moon for powers they won't share with us?

Erissa reaches the small rundown cottage by the pond, and the peacefulness of the surroundings struck her. The pond is calm and still, reflecting the greenery that surrounds it, and the air is thick with the sweet scent of wildflowers. The cottage itself is small and weathered, with faded white paint peeling off the wooden walls. Moss covered the roof, and the windows are small and slightly crooked, as if they were hand-made. A rickety wooden porch wraps around the front of the cottage, with a single rocking chair sitting in the corner.

As she steps inside, a cosy, rustic interior greets her. The walls are made of rough, exposed wood, and the floors are covered in faded, patterned rugs. A fireplace takes up most of the far wall, with a stack of firewood piled neatly beside it. The furniture is simple but functional, with a worn leather sofa and a small wooden table surrounded by mismatched chairs. The kitchen area is compact, with a small stove, a sink, and a few shelves stocked with basic supplies. Despite its rough exterior, the cottage has a certain charm and warmth that makes her feel right at home. And as she steps back outside and takes in the tranquil beauty of the pond and its surroundings, she can't help but feel a sense of peace and contentment settle over her.

That feeling was soon gone as Erissa looks up and sees her parents standing in front of the hallway, arms crossed and faces stern.

"Why isn't breakfast ready?" Erissa's mom gripes. "We took you in as a baby out of the kindness of our hearts - and this is how we're repaid?"

Erissa flinches at her mother's tone, and bows her head in shame.

"It won't happen again, mum," Erissa quickly apologises and quickly sets the table. As Erissa finishes arranging the table, she takes a deep breath and approaches her parents, gesturing towards their seats. She silently signals that everything is ready, hoping to convey her sincere apology through her actions. Her parents, albeit impatiently, take their seats, awaiting their morning meal. Despite the tension in the air, Erissa remains determined to make things right and restore harmony to their morning routine.

She moves swiftly and purposefully in the kitchen, carefully arranging plates of steaming pancakes, bowls of fresh fruit, and cups of aromatic coffee on the table. The clinking of cutlery and the inviting aroma fill the air, as Erissa's hands work diligently to transform ingredients into a comforting meal. Despite the lingering tension, she pours her love and remorse into each dish, hoping that the sight and taste of the breakfast will convey her sincere apology to her adoptive parents.

Erissa's parents, having finished their breakfast, stand up from the table, signalling their readiness to venture into the nearby village. Her mother retrieves her purse, ensuring she has all the essentials for their outing, while her father adjusts his coat, ready to face the brisk morning air. They give Erissa a nod before heading out of the house.

Erissa couldn't help but let out a heavy sigh, feeling the weight of her parents' disapproval lingering in the air. She thought their disapproving glances and criticisms were as predictable and constant as the moon rising each night. No matter how hard she tried to mend their relationship or prove herself, it felt as though she was constantly falling short of their expectations. The sigh carried both resignation and a hint of sadness, as Erissa yearned for a sense of acceptance and understanding from her adoptive parents.

What could make them see me in a different light? Erissa wondered to herself gloomily.

But after that thought, an idea took hold…

ERISSA

After picking up the remnants of the breakfast her parents had enjoyed, Erissa washes the dishes and carefully dries them. Now that the home is cleaned, it is time to tend to the farm. Pulling her honey-coloured hair in a loose bun, Erissa walks towards the front door and grabs the large wicker basket lying next to her shoes. She steps out into the yard and takes stock of her environment. The midmorning sky stretches out in a captivating display of clear, azure blue, dotted here and there with fluffy white clouds. The air carries a subtle scent of freshly bloomed flowers and lush greenery, invigorating the senses. Nature is vibrant and alive, the vibrant hues of emerald-green leaves dance in the gentle breeze, rustling ever so softly. Birds chirp melodiously, serenading the world with their delightful songs. A sense of tranquillity washes over Erissa as she walks barefoot on the soft, dew-kissed grass. The earth feels cool beneath her feet, providing a refreshing contrast to the warm air. With the sun shining brightly overhead, casting its golden glow on everything it touches, time seems to slow down. But it's not a morning of leisure and relaxation.

Erissa carefully lets herself into the shabby chicken coop, careful not to startle the hens. Her first step is ensuring that there was enough feed available for the hens and that the containers are clean and in good condition. Moving carefully among the hens, Erissa checks the nesting boxes for any eggs that have been laid. She gently retrieves the eggs, being cautious not to disturb the hens or accidentally break any eggs in the process. Leaving the coop, Erissa ensures that the door and other openings are sealed to protect the hens from potential predators. The hens cluck contently as Erissa re-latches the front gate.

Wiping the dirt from her hands, Erissa walks around the small pond and steps over the small chicken-wire fence that guards the family's modest vegetable garden. Erissa spends a short time watering the plants, pulling the weeds, and ensuring they are well cared for.

Erissa, with her deep affection for milking the cows and tending to the larger livestock, often reserves these tasks for the end of her day. This deliberate choice allows her to savour the experience and dedicate her undivided attention to the animals. She finds solace in the rhythmic movements and the connection she forms with each individual animal under her care.

Erissa enters the barn, welcomed by the familiar scents and sounds of her beloved cows. Their gentle lowing and the rustling of straw create a peaceful ambiance that soothes her spirit. With practised ease, she fetches the necessary equipment, ensuring everything is clean and ready for use.

Approaching the first cow, Erissa establishes a bond of trust, speaking softly and gently stroking the animal's flank. She expertly pulls up a small wooden stool and begins milking, commencing a rhythmic process that has become second nature to her. The cow, accustomed to Erissa's touch, seems at ease, providing her with nourishing milk that will soon find its way into the homes and hearts of those who depend on it.

Erissa's love for her work extends beyond milking alone. She takes pride in the well-being of her family's livestock, recognizing the importance of their comfort and health. After completing the milking routine, she attentively checks each animal, ensuring they have ample food, clean water, and comfortable resting areas. She meticulously inspects them for any signs of illness or distress, ready to offer aid and support if needed.

As darkness settles over the farm, Erissa leaves the barn with a sense of contentment. The tasks she has saved for last have served as a reminder of her purpose and passion. Her commitment to nurturing and supporting the livestock brings her fulfilment, and she eagerly awaits the following day's opportunity to repeat the cycle of care, knowing that her cherished task of milking the cows and tending to the animals will always hold a special place in her heart.

As Erissa walks back home after completing her daily tasks, she starts thinking about the dinner she will prepare for her parents. She knows they will be returning from the village soon and will want to have a delicious and satisfying meal ready for them.

Walking inside, Erissa enters the kitchen and assesses the ingredients available. She decides to prepare a hearty vegetable stew accompanied by freshly baked bread. She starts by chopping an assortment of vegetables including carrots, potatoes, bell peppers, and onions. While the vegetables simmer in a pot on the stove, Erissa moves on to prepare the bread dough. After letting it rise for some time, she shapes the dough into small individual loaves and places them in the oven to bake. With the stew and bread underway, Erissa takes a moment to set the table, making sure everything is arranged neatly and adding a vase with fresh flowers as a pleasant touch. She pours two glasses of water and sets them on the table.

As the aroma of the stew and bread fills the house, Erissa glances at the clock and realises her parents will arrive soon. She tidies up the kitchen, making sure all the utensils and ingredients are put away. Erissa hurriedly makes her way to the washroom, determined to eliminate the unpleasant odour clinging to her.

She closes the door behind her, hoping to contain any lingering scent. Looking at herself in the mirror, she realises that her appearance has also been affected by her time spent outside. Her tan had deepened on her toned body, and her hazel eyes were slightly bloodshot from tiredness from her long day. She pulls a few errant pieces of straw from her shoulder-length yellow hair, and quickly scrubbed the filth of the day from her tired body. Donning a long cotton sleep shirt, Erissa pads back to the kitchen, where she sees both parents asleep on the couch. The dinner has been eaten in full, and Erissa regrets not having eaten a little of the meal before her parents got home. She grabs some dried fruit from a jar on the counter and quietly cleans up the table before slipping undetected out into the cool summer night.

As Erissa briskly makes her way through the forest, the setting sun casts long shadows across the towering trees, creating a mystical ambiance. The transition from day to night only enhances the beauty of her surroundings. As darkness slowly envelops the forest, a symphony of nocturnal sounds emerges. The rustling leaves whisper secrets, and the hooting of an owl echoes in the distance, adding an ethereal touch to the atmosphere. The air becomes cooler, and the scents of the forest take on a distinct character, earthy and rich.

Erissa quickens her pace, eager to witness the transformation of the forest under the moonlit sky. She ventures deeper into the woods, noticing how the stars gentle glow filtered through the branches, casting an otherworldly illumination on the forest floor. Fireflies danced among the foliage, their luminous bodies creating a whimsical spectacle that captivates Erissa's gaze.

With silent footsteps, Erissa deftly manoeuvres past the towering noble fir tree that stands as a guardian along her path. She feels an anticipation building within her, urging her to quicken her pace and witness the moon's unveiling once again. The desire to behold the enchanting sight motivates her, propelling her through the forest with a renewed energy. As she presses onward, her steps become more swift, her heart pounding in rhythm with her quickened pace. The forest seemed to sense her eagerness, for the moon peeked through the gaps in the dense foliage, casting a soft glow on the surrounding landscape.

Erissa stands still, absorbing the breathtaking scene before her. The moon's radiance highlights the intricate details of the trees, casting elongated shadows that dance upon the forest floor. It is a moment of serene beauty.

Nestling into a thick tuft of tall grass, it disappointed Erissa to see she missed the raising of the moon by the magnificent swan.

No matter, Erissa thinks to herself. My plan will still be a success.

Getting comfortable, she naps in short bursts. With each passing hour, the moon brings itself closer and closer back to Earth, and Erissa finds herself unable to rest any longer. Her plan is almost ready. There is no backing out now. Erissa watches in awe as the wispy blonde fae, with an air of tranquillity, approaches the large tree with the moon cradled gently in her arms. The fae's delicate wings shimmer with a soft iridescence, reflecting the moon's ethereal light, as they slowly retract back in her body.

As the fae reaches the tree, she places the moon in a hollow at the base of its trunk, like a precious offering to the natural world. The tree, ancient and wise, seems to come alive with a gentle hum, as if acknowledging the celestial orb.

Erissa senses a profound connection between the fae, the tree, and the moon—a harmonious relationship that transcends the boundaries of the dream realm. She feels drawn to approach them, compelled by an inexplicable force. With a serene smile, Erissa watches the fae turn away, bidding farewell to the hidden sanctuary.

As the fae starts her journey back, Erissa follows her gaze, taking in the field of freshly replanted stars. The stars, like seeds sown in the celestial soil, emit a soft glow, twinkling in the dark expanse above. It is a testament to the fae's efforts, ensuring that the night sky remains adorned with its celestial tapestry.

Not allowing for even a second of hesitation, Erissa dashes to the hiding spot and scoops up the now palm-sized moon.

ERISSA

$\mathcal{E}$rissa approaches her family's cottage, her footsteps heavy with fatigue. As she reaches the front door, she notices her parents standing there, their expressions clouded with disappointment. However, their faces quickly transform into a mix of surprise and greed as they catch sight of the tiny orb she clasps in her hands.

"Erissa, is that... the moon?" her father asks, his voice filled with astonishment.

Erissa nods softly, holding her hands out in front of him. His eyes widened, and he delicately grasped the luminescent sphere.

"Do you know what this means?" he says excitedly. "The Fae will have to share their secrets with us now! We have the ultimate bargaining chip." Erissa's father was almost manic, pacing throughout the compact living room.

Erissa spoke up, ecstatic at her parents' approval.

"Shall I come with you to the village centre, father?" she looks up at her dad with hope in her caramel eyes. "They'll be so pleased to see what I've done for our town!"

Erissa's father's expression darkens as he fixes his gaze on her. The excitement that once filled the room dissipates, replaced by a sense of unease. His voice takes on a stern tone as he replies to her suggestion.

"That would be unwise, Erissa," he spoke firmly. "You know how the villagers feel about you. This will change nothing."

Erissa tries to fight back tears, and there is a lump in her throat that won't go down. As her eyes well up, her mother whispers.

"When we found you, you were just a baby," she said. "As we approached the outskirts of Thornbrook, our attention was drawn to a faint sound. Curiosity piqued, they followed the gentle cries until we discovered a small bundle nestled among the foliage. Our hearts skipped a beat as we realised it was a baby swaddled in a soft blanket. That baby was you." She breathed in and continued.

"We took you in, despite knowing that you may have Fae lineage... The townspeople could not accept you, no matter how human you appeared, or may be. But as you've gotten older, no special talents have manifested. It seems you are just an average human. The villagers will still not accept you, regardless of your offering. They will only see it as a trap set by you and the Fae, collaborating," Erissa's mother finishes.

"Are the Fae really that wicked?" Erissa speaks up, looking to her parents for clarification.

Her father, standing near the small side table near the couch, slams his fist on the already delicate wood, splitting it in half.

"They are scum!" He yelled loudly. "Worthless scum, keeping their power to themselves and letting the rest of us suffer. They have no regard for human life, manipulating and deceiving us for their own selfish gains. They play with our lives like we're mere toys to them. Don't be fooled, Erissa. The Fae may appear charming and beautiful, but their intentions are always sinister. They lure unsuspecting humans into their realm, enchant them, and then cast them aside like discarded playthings. They are not to be trusted."

Frightened, Erissa nods at her enraged father.

Satisfied at her compliance, her father smooths his hair and takes a deep, calming breath.

"I know just how to speak to our townspeople about this new discovery. Dear, come with me while we make this marvellous announcement. Erissa, we still expect your daily chores to be finished by the time we return home, and a hearty dinner prepared, considering your failure to serve breakfast this morning."

Erissa, still unwilling to speak lest she triggers her father's rage again, simply nods and stares at her feet. She hears footsteps, followed by the sound of the front door opening and closing. She breathes a sigh of relief and quickly changes into her coveralls. Stepping outside, she finds a shady spot beneath a towering tree, its branches extending like open arms, providing a respite from the already sultry morning. The coolness of the shade envelopes her, and she takes a moment to sit down, absorbing the peaceful ambiance.

Agitated clucking could be heard from the coop across from Erissa, and she slowly rises to her feet.

"I'm coming, ladies," Erissa smiles and walks toward the henhouse.

As she approaches the henhouse, she can see a group of chickens huddled together near the entrance, their feathers ruffled and their movements agitated. The clucking grows louder and more frantic as she gets closer, showing that something was amiss.

Erissa gently pushes open the door to the coop, and a wave of warm, earthy scents greet her. Inside, she sees her beloved flock of hens bustling about, their beady eyes flicking nervously. Their feathers, usually neat and preened, appear dishevelled, and their usual contented clucks are replaced with anxious squawks.

Curiosity and concern fill Erissa's heart as she scans the coop for any signs of trouble. She carefully moves toward the distressed hens, her movements slow and deliberate to avoid startling them further. As she approaches, a flash of movement catches her eye near the nesting boxes. Peering closer, Erissa spots a small, slithering creature—an unwelcome visitor in the chicken coop. A snake, its sinuous body coiled near the eggs, had caused the commotion among the hens.

Understanding the source of their distress, Erissa knows she needs to act swiftly to protect her feathery friends and restore their sense of security.

Erissa skillfully manoeuvres a stick that was close by, guiding the snake away from the nesting boxes and toward the exit of the coop. She maintains a respectful distance, ensuring the snake has a clear path to slither away and find a more suitable habitat. As the snake leaves the coop, a sense of relief seems to ripple through the flock. The hens gradually calm down, their clucking subsiding into a more tranquil chorus. Erissa watches them closely, observing their behaviour to ensure they feel secure once again.

That was enough excitement for today, Erissa thinks as she wipes the sweat from her brow.

Erissa moves efficiently through her chores, tending to her beloved cows with care and dedication. As she enters the barn, the familiar scent of hay and the gentle lowing of the cows greet her. Their large, gentle eyes met hers with a sense of trust and familiarity. With a warm smile on her face, Erissa approaches each cow, giving them each a few extra chin scratches and gentle pats on their sturdy backs. The cows lean into her touch, relishing the affection and connection they share. It is a moment of mutual appreciation and comfort—a simple exchange of love and gratitude between human and animal. Satisfied that her cows are content and well-cared for, Erissa bid them farewell, promising to return soon. She knows they will spend the rest of the day leisurely grazing in the lush green pasture, enjoying the warmth of the sun on their backs.

With a sense of fulfilment, Erissa makes her way back to the worn cottage that she calls home. She dons an apron, her hands deftly moving across the counter-tops as she gathers ingredients and prepares a delicious meal. The rhythmic sounds of chopping, sizzling, and stirring fill the air as Erissa immerses herself in the culinary creation. Her mind wanders to the peaceful moments she had experienced throughout the day—the satisfaction of tending to her animals, the beauty of the countryside, and the harmonious connection with nature.

Her parents enter just as Erissa is placing the finishing touches on the apology meal.

"This smells great, Erissa," her mother compliments. Her father nods at her mother's sentiments and tucks into the meal.

After clearing the table, Erissa's parents retire to the living room, and her mother stokes the fire in the wood-burning fireplace. They settle into their favourite armchairs, enjoying the warmth and subtle sounds of crackles and pops. As the fire continues to burn, casting a warm glow on the walls, Erissa inches her way over to the dark green threadbare rug.

"The townspeople are pleased," her father boasts to the room. "We meet tomorrow to discuss how to best extort the Fae," he finishes.

Quietly, Erissa stood up from the rug and made her

way closer to her parents, her expression filled with concern.

"Father," she speaks softly, "is it wise to provoke the Fae? They possess great magic, and they could retaliate if they feel threatened or wronged."

Her mother paused in her task of stoking the fire and glances at Erissa with a mix of surprise and worry. "We have been waiting for an opportunity such as this for years," her mother admonishes her.

"I do not wish to speak of this again, Erissa," her father interjects calmly but loudly. There is a glint in his eyes that suggests a disagreement is not in Erissa's best interests.

She nods meekly and sits on the rug once again. As her parents relax by the fire, they are startled by a piercing howl that seemed to emanate from the east. The Fae had discovered the missing moon.

CALIDA

I gather my sisters, and we scour the forest. We overturn rocks, rummage through foliage, and examine every nook and cranny, searching for clues or signs of a disturbance. As we explore deeper into the forest, our senses heighten, attuned to the subtle sounds and sights of nature around us. We keep our eyes peeled for any trace of our quarry, whether it's footprints, broken branches, or disturbed undergrowth. Every peculiar noise or rustle makes our hearts skip a beat, hoping it might lead us closer to our objective.

The forest teems with life, providing us with a myriad of distractions and challenges. We encounter an array of the local wildlife, from curious squirrels darting through the branches to birds chirping melodiously overhead, though they could not give us any insight on our search. Despite these enchanting distractions, we remain focused on our mission, keeping our search methodical and thorough.

It is really time to panic now. The moon is officially missing.

Did I not properly put it away? I wonder to myself, my heart racing from the stress.

The possibility that I might have neglected to properly put something as important as this away gnaws at me. I take a moment to breathe deeply and regain my composure. I try to remember that mistakes can happen to anyone, and it's crucial not to let self-doubt consume me. The memory of placing the moon in its usual spot inside the hollow tree resurfaces in my mind. Nothing seemed amiss, and the day carried on as usual.

Though the stars have already been cast in the night sky by my sisters, the missing moon weighs heavily on our minds and hearts. One night may not make much of a difference, but if the moon is not recovered soon, the delicate balance of nature and the celestial rhythm will be disrupted - affecting tides, ecosystems, and even human lives.

With this realisation, my sense of urgency intensifies. My sisters and I understand the gravity of the situation and the need to find the missing moon promptly. The weight on our minds and hearts fuels my determination to search with renewed vigour. As our spirits waver, we glimpse something peculiar—a scrap of cobalt-blue fabric half-buried in the nearby undergrowth. Rushing towards it, we uncover what appears to be a piece of cloak, not belonging to any of us. My heart races with anticipation, realising that an intruder was in our midst this morning.

A sister with the transformative power of a black bear inches forward to the cloth and takes a deep sniff. Her face is inquisitive, inhaling the scent that clings to the fabric. The rest of us watch in anticipation, holding your breath, hoping that her keen sense of smell will provide a clue or lead in the search for the missing moon.

After what feels like an eternity, my sister's pupils dilate and she gasps. "Mortal," she chokes out.

It feels as if someone suddenly laced my veins with ice water. It sends a shiver down my spine, and an almost imperceptible chill permeates the surrounding air. The sudden and unexpected change in my physical sensation catches me off guard, leaving me unsettled.

I take a deep breath and try to ground myself in the present moment. Acknowledging the icy sensation and allowing myself to observe it.

"Are you sure?" I ask, but I already know her answer.

She nods slightly, her eyes still wide. A prolonged pause took hold until one of the younger Fae let out a piercing scream.

"We must sort this out," an older Fae commanded. "Search and protect our realm."

The Fae with the ability to transform into flying animals take to the sky in search of answers, their wings beating with determination. They soar gracefully through their domain, exploring every nook and cranny, searching for any signs or clues related to the missing moon.

Their keen eyesight and agility allow them to navigate the intricate web of the forest with ease. They dart between trees, glide over shimmering streams, and hover near delicate blossoms, hoping to uncover a hidden truth that might lead them closer to the moon's whereabouts.

I wiped an errant tear from my eye, trying to stay strong for my sisters. I cannot help but feel this is my fault, and my breaths quicken. The weight of responsibility settles upon my shoulders, and a sense of guilt permeates my thoughts. The older Fae that got my sisters organised comes up to me and brings my hands delicately to her own.

"It's important to acknowledge these feelings without allowing them to consume you. Remember that mistakes and unforeseen circumstances can happen to anyone, and it is not solely your burden to bear. The search for the missing moon is a collective effort, and your sisters are here to support you just as you support them. Take a moment to focus on your breath, allowing it to slow and steady your racing heart. Inhale deeply, feeling the air fill your lungs, and exhale slowly, releasing any tension or self-blame you may be holding onto. Remind yourself that you are doing your best in a challenging situation, and that is all anyone can ask of you. It's natural to question your actions and wonder if there was something you could have done differently. However, dwelling on self-blame will only hinder your ability to think clearly and make progress. Instead, channel your energy into productive and positive actions," she finished softly.

I smiled at her, thankful for her honesty and optimism. Allowing my breaths to slow and deepen, I feel better and can think more clearly.

"Right then," I sniffle. "Let's get our moon back before it's too late."

"That's the spirit," the elder smiled at me encouragingly. "I knew your mum, and she would be proud of the woman you've become - mistake or not. But this is not your mistake, dear. A human did this. This human has gravely underestimated the power we share. We will return the moon to its rightful place, and these foolish mortals will be dealt with swiftly and severely."

*E*rissa's parents smile at each other upon hearing the Fae in such agony over the missing moon. The sounds of panicked cries could be heard clearly from the family's living room, and it felt as if the Fae were right outside their small home. Loud noises could be heard from outside, interrupting the tranquillity of the night. Erissa's parents exchange excited glances as they rush to the window to investigate the commotion.

Outside, a chaotic scene unfolds as Fae creatures of various sizes and shapes darted through the mostly darkened sky. Their wings fluttered frantically, their cries filled with anguish and despair. It appeared the entire Fae realm had descended into panic over the disappearance of the moon. The Fae flew erratically, crashing into each other, buildings, and trees in their desperate search for answers. The absence of the moon had disrupted their natural order, leaving them lost and in agony.

"You see this?" Erissa's father grins at the chaos. "This is all thanks to you!" For once, he smiles at his adopted daughter and marvels at the sight.

Erissa smiles back uneasily, but shakes away her discomfort. Having her parents' approval means everything to her. She understands they are embarking on a dangerous journey, but she can't help feeling a mix of worry and excitement for what lay ahead.

As the first light of dawn spreads across the land, the Fae retire back to the wilds empty handed. Erissa is told to keep the moon hidden under her bed until it is needed - her parents feel that a child's room would be the last place one would look for such a valuable arte-fact. The young girl dutifully obeys her parents' instructions, tucking the moon carefully under her bed, ensuring it remains hidden from searching eyes. Erissa can't help but daydreams about the possibilities that lie within that glowing orb. The stories she has heard of the Fae and their magical realms captivate her imagina-tion, igniting a yearning within her to explore the enchanting world hidden from mortal eyes.

Erissa, determined to regain her usual morning routine, pads quietly to the washroom. The cool wood beneath her feet provides a gentle reminder of the familiar and grounds her in the present moment. Entering the washroom, she approaches the sink and catches her reflection in the mirror. Her eyes still held a glimmer of excitement, but she is determined to set it aside for the time being. She reaches for her toothbrush and applies a dab of toothpaste, focusing on the rhythmic motions of brushing her teeth. As the bristles move against her teeth, Erissa allows herself to fully engage with the sensation, feeling the cleansing action and the fresh minty taste in her mouth. With each stroke, she lets go of the lingering excitement and embraces the simplicity of the task at hand. Once she finishes brushing her teeth, Erissa splashes cold water on her face. The coolness refreshes her skin and brings her back to the present moment. She takes a moment to appreciate the feeling of the water against her skin, letting it wash away any traces of restlessness or distraction.

Erissa takes a deep breath and meets her own gaze in the mirror. She acknowledges the excitement that still lingers within her, but makes a conscious decision to set it aside for now. Today is about finding stability, routine, and regaining her usual sense of calm.

Leaving the washroom, Erissa continues with her morning routine, knowing that the familiar activities will help ground her further. She changes into her comfortable attire, ties her hair back, and heads to the kitchen to prepare morning tea. As she prepares the Earl Grey, Erissa allows herself a few moments of quiet reflection, focusing on the soothing warmth of the cup in her hands. The steam rising from the tea seems to carry away the remnants of excitement, leaving her feeling more centred and ready to embrace the day.

Erissa prepares a light breakfast to pair with the tea.

She opens the cupboard and retrieves a large ceramic bowl, opting for a simple yet nourishing meal. Erissa reaches for a box of granola and sprinkles a generous amount into the bowl, savouring the sweet aroma that fills the air. She then adds a dollop of creamy yoghurt, allowing it to gently cascade over the granola, forming a delicious and satisfying base for her breakfast.

She approaches the icebox and pulls out a container of fresh berries. She handpicks a handful of vibrant strawberries, plump blueberries, and juicy raspberries, placing them atop the yoghurt and granola. The burst of colours instantly lifts her spirits, adding a touch of natural sweetness to the morning meal. To complete her breakfast, Erissa grabs a drizzle of honey from the pantry. She delicately drizzles it over the bowl, watching as the golden liquid cascades down, enhancing the flavours and adding a touch of decadence to the dish.

Her parents sit at the table, still wiping the sleep from their eyes. Both parents acknowledge the effort Erissa had put into the meal, and she can't help but smile both inward and outward.

"Rest before you take care of the outside duties, yeah?" her mother offers her for the first time she can ever remember.

Her father looks up from his meal, hesitating, but ultimately nods towards Erissa.

Entering her room, Erissa closes the door behind her, shutting out the outside world. The familiar scent of her sanctuary envelopes her, bringing a sense of comfort and tranquillity. She walks over to her bed, adorned with soft pillows and a cosy lightweight quilt, inviting her to take a brief rest. Erissa allows herself to sink into the plush mattress filled with errant down from her geese, feeling the weight of the previous day beginning to lift from her shoulders. She closes her eyes and focuses on her breathing, allowing herself to enter a state of relaxation.

Erissa's eyes snap open as she hears a peculiar choking sound coming from outside her partially opened window. Concern on her face, she quickly sat up in bed, fully alert. She knows that something is amiss. Throwing off her covers, Erissa wastes no time. She hurriedly gets out of bed, her mind racing with thoughts about the source of the unusual sound. As she walks through the house, she notices her parents had already left for town, leaving her to handle the situation on her own. With determination and focus, Erissa makes her way to the hallway closet, where she keeps her working boots. She swiftly slides them on, lacing them up with practised efficiency.

As she makes her way to the front door, Erissa mentally prepares herself for the unknown. With a deep breath, she opens the door and steps outside. Searching for the source, Erissa follows her ears. The land is unusually silent, broken only by the occasional choked cough echoing in the distance.

Erissa's curiosity only grows as she follows the sound, her sturdy boots providing a steady rhythm against the uneven grass. The urgency in her steps matches the quickening beat of her heart. As she turns the corner, she expects to find something chaotic or distressing, but her eyes widen in surprise at the serene sight before her.

A solitary swan floats gracefully in the centre of the pond, its pure white feathers glistening in the sunlight. However, what caught Erissa's attention is the haunting sound emanating from the beautiful creature. It seems as if the swan is crying, its mournful calls filling the air.

Concern and empathy wells up within Erissa as she observes the swan's distress. She approaches the pond slowly, careful not to startle the elegant bird. Her eyes never leave the swan, captivated by its melancholic presence.

As she draws nearer, Erissa notices the swan's delicate movements. It appears to be struggling with something, occasionally dipping its head into the water as if searching for something precious it had lost. Erissa couldn't help but feel a deep connection to the swan's sorrow.

With a gentle and cautious demeanour, Erissa kneels at the edge of the pond, her gaze locking with the swan's. She offers soothing words, speaking in a hushed tone, hoping to provide comfort to the distressed creature.

Reaching out with one hand, Erissa extends her palm towards the swan, as if offering solace and understanding. The swan pauses, its cries momentarily ceasing, and regards her with curious eyes.

As Erissa takes a step forward, her intention to offer

comfort and understanding to the swan is met with an unexpected crack of a branch under her boot. The loud sound reverberates through the stillness, startling both Erissa and the swan.

In an instant, the graceful creature takes flight, its majestic wings unfurling with a powerful beat. Erissa's heart sinks as she watches the swan soar into the sky, tears streaming down its beak once again. The sight fills her with a mixture of curiosity and worry, wondering what could cause such profound pain in such a beautiful and ethereal creature.

CALIDA

As I ponder the encounter with the young girl, her kindness lingers in my thoughts. Though her age seemed tender, there was an undeniable wisdom that emanated from her eyes, defying the limits of her years. It was as if she held within her a reservoir of experience and understanding that surpassed the bounds of mortal existence.

Her act of kindness had touched me deeply, resonating within my soul. In a world often consumed by self-interest and indifference, encountering such genuine compassion was a rare treasure. It reminded me that kindness knows no age or boundaries, and that even the youngest among us can possess a profound understanding of the human condition.

In my darkest hour, that mortal girl offered a rare kindness.

Although I wonder if she would have been as kind knowing I am a Fae, I think to myself morosely.

I fly back to the wilds, not eager to tell my sisters I still have not located the moon. My sisters listen intently, their expressions filled with understanding and empathy.

"This is not your fault!" They speak in unison.

But I can't help but feel they are wrong. My one task, once the moon has completed its round in the night sky, is ensuring its safety.

I ponder over the reasons behind my doubts. *Is it because I believe I could have done something differently?*

Taking a moment to reflect, I consider the vastness of the universe and the countless factors that can affect celestial bodies like the moon. While I have been assigned ensuring its safety, perhaps it's important to acknowledge that there are limitations to what any individual can control. I remind myself that mistakes and unforeseen events can happen, even with the best intentions and efforts. It is essential to learn from these experiences, adapt our approaches, and continue striving to fulfil our tasks to the best of our abilities.

I take a deep breath and centre myself before turning to my sisters.

"This is not something we can let slide, though." I look at each one of them and the seriousness of the situation is palpable.

"Without the moon, our world will be forever altered," I continue, my voice filled with determination.

"Its absence would disrupt the delicate balance of tides, and affect ecosystems," I finish.

As my words hang in the air, my sister's nod in agreement, their expressions mirroring my resolve. They understand the gravity of the situation and the significance of our role in safeguarding the moon. While the burden of responsibility remains, we find solace in our united front, knowing that we are not alone in our commitment. The safety of the moon becomes a shared mission, and we draw strength from the support and expertise of one another.

"What can we do next?" a younger Fae that had been tending to the eggs in the poultry yard looked up from her duties.

As I hesitate, the guardian Fae Nettelia rushes into our planning circle.

"A human delivered this at the base of our tree," she panted, out of breath. "The message does not bode well for us," she breathed out and sat down.

With a shaky hand, Nettelia hands me the rolled up parchment.

CALIDA

I am writing to bring to your attention a matter of utmost urgency and importance. As of two days prior, I have successfully taken control of the Moon and currently hold it hostage until our demands are met.

Before I proceed, I want to clarify that my intentions are not malicious or harmful. I understand the implications and consequences of such actions and I am prepared to negotiate in a peaceful manner.

We acknowledge the extraordinary powers and additional abilities possessed by the Fae and firmly believe in the existence of this magic that is being concealed from us. If you do not disclose your secrets, we will deprive you of witnessing the moon ever again. You have until the week's end to fulfil our requirements.

* * *

As the words from the parchment escape my lips, I study my sisters' expressions. Their faces contort with fury and shock, their emotions impossible to miss. The atmosphere instantly becomes charged as everyone in the room speaks simultaneously, their voices filled with outrage and indignation.

Amidst the clamour, I struggle to make out individual words as the collective anger reverberates through the air. It's a tumultuous moment, with each sister voicing her concerns and grievances with varying degrees of intensity. The forest pulses with the weight of our emotions, and it's clear that the contents of the parchment have struck a deep chord within each of us.

"We are born this way, our magic cannot be taught!" One shouted.

"We will never see the moon again!" Another wailed.

I watch as their gestures become more animated, their voices growing louder in an attempt to be heard over one another. The air crackles with tension as conflicting opinions clash, echoing off the walls of the room.

The elder's authoritative voice cuts through the chaos, demanding silence. "Enough!" she exclaims, and the room falls into hushed stillness.

A call for reason and unity emerges from the Elder's lips, breaking through the heated atmosphere. "Let us gather our thoughts and approach this situation with rationality," she urges, her words carrying a sense of urgency. "If we succumb to division, the mortals have already claimed victory."

As the Elder's words sink in, a collective murmur of agreement ripples through me and my sisters. Though an undercurrent of unease lingers, it is clear to all that action must be taken. The looming sense of dread serves as a powerful motivator to work towards a common goal.

Amid this shared understanding, a tacit agreement emerges among us. It is time to formulate a plan—a strategy that will allow you to navigate the challenges ahead. The gravity of the situation weighs heavily, but the determination to overcome it fuels our collective resolve.

With a renewed sense of purpose, we prepare to gather our thoughts, pooling our ideas and strengths. The path ahead may be treacherous, but together, I know we stand ready to face whatever lies in wait, forging a plan that will counter the mortals' advancements and safeguard our realm.

It's decided that I will be the one to try to get the mortals to see reason. Because I am the one entrusted with raising and lowering the moon, perhaps I can explain to the villagers just how important it is to daily life for humans and Fae alike. My role as a mediator between these worlds grants me a certain credibility and perspective that might sway the mortals to see reason.

Armed with this knowledge and entrusted with a crucial mission, I accept the weight of the task ahead. It is up to me to convey the interdependence of the moon and how it contributes to the harmony between both realms. My ability to articulate the importance of this celestial body may prove instrumental in averting further conflict and fostering a sense of understanding between the mortals and the Fae.

A wave of apprehension washes over me as the weight of my impending task settles upon my shoulders. It is only natural to feel a mix of nervousness and uncertainty when faced with such a significant responsibility. The stakes are high, and the outcome of my efforts could have far-reaching consequences for both of the realms.

"It is in these moments of unease that your true strength and resilience are tested. Acknowledge and embrace your apprehension, for it is a reminder of the importance of your mission. Allow yourself a moment to gather your thoughts, breathe deeply, and find solace knowing that you are not alone. Draw upon the support and wisdom of your sisters and the Fae community, as their presence can offer you guidance and reassurance," the elder spoke directly to me.

Her reassurance calms me enough to take a few much-needed breaths, and I smile at her gratefully.

The weight of an additional challenge settles upon my thoughts as I consider the next hurdle: explaining the inherent nature of Fae magic. It becomes apparent that conveying the concept of innate magical abilities may prove to be an arduous task. I express your frustration with a sigh, a sense of helplessness looming over me.

Indeed, the concept of inherited magic is deeply

ingrained in the fabric of our being, an intrinsic part of Fae existence. It is not something that can be shared or taught, as it is an inherent gift bestowed upon you by birth. Communicating this understanding to the mortals, who may lack the frame of reference or the capacity to comprehend such concepts, poses a significant challenge.

Understanding the significance of the challenge ahead, my sisters nod in agreement, their expressions reflecting a shared determination.

With a collective understanding, a plan takes shape. The combined wisdom and insights of your sisters weave together, creating a tapestry of strategies and approaches. Each contribution adds a new thread, strengthening the overall fabric of your plan.

As we continue to refine and solidify your plan, a renewed sense of purpose and optimism fills the room. The daunting challenge ahead remains, but with the collective strength and ingenuity of my sisterhood, we have fortified ourselves for the task at hand. United in purpose. We stand ready to embark on this crucial journey, determined to bridge the gap and safeguard the delicate balance between the mortal realm and the realm of the Fae.

ERISSA

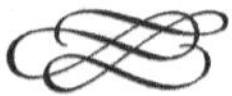

$\mathcal{E}$rissa discreetly observes the gathering of the Fae, her heart pounding with excitement and curiosity. The glimmering forest serves as the backdrop to their clandestine meeting, and a sense of enchantment fills the air. As she scans the group, one particular Fae captivates her attention—a familiar and stunningly beautiful blonde with ethereal grace.

The blonde Fae stands tall, her radiant presence enhanced by the starlight through the canopy. Her golden tresses cascaded in gentle waves down her back, shimmering with an otherworldly glow. Her eyes, a mesmerising shade of sapphire, sparkled with a mixture of wisdom and mischievousness. She exuded an aura of confidence and elegance that was hard to ignore, even with worry clear on her face.

Erissa's intrigue deepens as she notices the intensity of the Fae's discussion revolving around the missing moon. While she cannot discern the exact words being exchanged, the urgency and seriousness in their gestures and expressions are unmistakable. The blonde Fae, in particular, seems to take a central role in the conversation, her commanding presence and focused demeanour clear to Erissa, even from a distance. Her expressive eyes sparkle with concern, and her gestures convey a sense of determination and purpose.

Erissa continues to observe the Fae's passionate discussion about the missing moon, her initial thrill and excitement slowly transforms into a sense of empathy and concern. The gravity of the situation sinks in, and she realises that the Fae's distress is not something to rejoice in, but a genuine struggle that affects their entire existence.

Erissa's initial reaction stems from a curiosity fueled by the allure of the Fae's world. However, as she witnesses their heartfelt expressions and gestures, she see's the missing moon has brought about a deep turmoil within their realm. The Fae's connection to the moon is intertwined with their magic, their balance, and perhaps even their very survival.

A wave of compassion washes over Erissa as she contemplates the implications of the missing moon on the Fae and their way of life. She understands that what she initially perceived as an opportunity is, in reality, a crisis that threatened their harmony and well-being.

What did I do? Erissa thinks to herself.

Did I make a horrible mistake?

As Erissa continues to observe the Fae and their

distress over the missing moon, an overwhelming sense of guilt and regret wash over her. A deep realisation dawns upon her—a revelation that she herself is responsible the absence of the moon. In a desperate attempt to gain her parents' approval, she had committed a selfish act without considering the consequences it would have on others.

The weight of her actions bear heavily upon Erissa's conscience. She had allowed her ambition and desire for recognition to blind her to the potential harm she could inflict upon an entire realm. The pain and anguish reflected in the eyes of the Fae serves as a constant reminder of her thoughtlessness.

Regret floods Erissa's heart, mingling with a deep sense of remorse. She realises she has disrupted the delicate balance of the Fae's world and is causing them immeasurable distress. The once-thrilling prospect of involvement in their affairs now feels tainted by her own selfishness.

In the face of her remorse, Erissa's focus shifts from her own desires to the desperate need for redemption. She resolves to rectify her mistakes and restore the missing moon, regardless of the consequences it might entail for herself. The quest for her parents' approval has led her down a dark path, but she is determined to make amends and right the wrong she has committed.

She slowly backs away, careful not to disturb the Fae. The undergrowth is tricky to navigate, but she maintains her balance and avoid stepping on any delicate plants or unseen creatures. She casts occasional glances over her shoulder, half-expecting to see the Fae watching her from between the trees. But the forest remains quiet, as if holding its breath. The starlight filters through the canopy, casting dappled shadows on the forest floor. The scents of damp earth, wildflowers, and ancient trees mingle in the air, creating an intoxicating aroma that stirs her senses.

I can't let the sky go without the moon even one more night, she thinks to herself with determination.

Erissa reaches the cottage and sees the lights on inside, which show her parents are still awake. She walks in, and her parents greet her warmly from their spots on the couch. Her mother is knitting what looks to be a small blanket, and her father is writing on a bit of parchment. Erissa swallows nervously, not sure how to tell her parents about her change of heart.

Erissa takes a deep breath, summoning her courage. She knows that living an authentic life means honouring her true desires, even if they diverge from what others may expect of her. She approaches the conversation with honesty and vulnerability, hoping that her parents will understand and support her journey.

Her face flushes slightly, realising that her attempt to compose herself had inadvertently drawn attention to her emotional state. She quickly tries to reassure them, her voice slightly shaky but determined.

"Come here, sweetheart. What's been bothering you? You know you can talk to us about anything," her mother offers.

Erissa gives her mum a half-smile before speaking in a rush.

"We need to give the moon back. The Fae cannot share magic with us, and if we go without the moon for much longer, we could irreparably damage our world and theirs," she finishes her sentence and looks at her parents expectantly.

Her mother's mouth hangs open, and her eyes are wide. Her father is breathing heavily and his face is reddening. He stands abruptly, his parchment and quill falling to the ground, and Erissa flinches.

"We will do no such thing!" Her father roars.

"But-" Erissa tries to explain.

"If you're not with us, you are against us. Is this what you want, Erissa?" he asks his adopted daughter, still breathing heavily.

"Father, this is not right. I stole the moon without knowing the repercussions it would cause. I-"

"You are no child of mine! We will get the answers we seek, with or without you - you insolent fool!"

Erissa's father angrily strides over to her and grabs her by the hair, dragging her to her room. He tosses her inside, where she smacks the bedframe and yelps. Her adoptive father pays no attention to her, and he grasps around under her bed until the moon is found. He grips it tightly in his hand and walks back to the entrance of Erissa's room.

"You will remain here until you see the error of your ways," her father growls out before slamming the door behind him.

CALIDA

I am calm now that a plan is in place. My sisters help me dress, draping me in flowing fabrics of vibrant colours. The delicate silk wraps around my body, caressing my skin with a gentle touch. The hues of emerald green, sapphire blue, and ruby red intertwine, creating a mesmerising tapestry that reflects the essence of my spirit.

As my sisters carefully fasten the intricate clasps and tie the silk ribbons, I feel a sense of empowerment enveloping me. Each knot tied represents a connection, a bond between us, strengthening our unity as we embark on this journey together.

The fabric cascades down in graceful folds, embracing my every curve and accentuating the gracefulness of my movements. I feel like a majestic bird ready to take flight, spreading its wings and soaring across the vast expanse of the sky.

With each layer of fabric carefully draped, I am reminded of the layers of strength and resilience that live within me. The fabric becomes a shield against the uncertainties that lie ahead, a reminder of the beauty and courage that dwell in the depths of my being. I am ready to step forward into the world, radiating resilience, elegance, and the indomitable spirit of my sisters beside me.

I walk past my cottage, and the humble garden I tend to daily. It reminds me of simpler times, when the world seemed less complex and worries were few. The scent of blooming flowers wafts through the air, carrying with it a sense of tranquillity and nostalgia. Each step I take on the grass path evokes memories of planting seeds, nurturing tender sprouts, and witnessing nature's remarkable ability to flourish.With a grateful heart, I continue my journey, carrying the essence of the garden with me.

The tree standing tall at the entrance of the Hemlock Wilds welcomes me once again, its gnarled branches reaching towards the sky. As I approach, I can't help but feel a mix of anticipation and trepidation.

As I walk along the familiar path, I come across the tranquil pond where I sought solace in my swan-form during my initial search for the moon. The memory of that moment lingers in my mind, a reminder of the challenges I faced.I dip my hand into the cool water, feeling its gentle caress against my skin. It reminds me of the healing power of nature, its ability to soothe and rejuvenate. The water, once a symbol of sadness, now becomes a source of renewal and resilience. I see this body of water becoming a symbol of transformation, a space where I can shed the burdens of the past and embrace the untapped potential that lies within.

Amid my sombre thoughts, a soft sound catches my attention—a girl's gentle weeping. I remember the girl who offered me solace during my moments of despair. Her presence was a beacon of light, a reminder that even in the depths of sadness, there is the potential for connection, understanding, and support.

Is it the same girl? I wonder.

I am tempted to find her and offer solace, but my task is far too great to allow any distractions. The magnitude of this endeavour demands my full attention and energy. The safe return of the moon is my priority, and every step I take, every decision I make, is aligned with this goal. I remind myself of the profound impact that the moon's return will have on the lives of countless individuals, the restoration of natural rhythms and the guidance it provides in the darkest of nights.

I continue my walk to the town square, and in moments of doubt or temptation, I ground myself with the purpose that fuels my determination. I draw strength from the knowledge that, by fulfilling this mission, I am contributing to the well-being of the world and creating a future that holds hope, inspiration, and the potential for transformative change.

The town square, typically bustling with activity during the day, is now mostly empty, save for a few stray leaves swirling in the gentle breeze. The buildings that surround the square stand tall and silent, their windows displaying faint glimmers of light from within, showing the early risers preparing for the day ahead.

The absence of the moon adds an eerie element to the scene. Without its usual soft glow, the night sky appears unusually dark, with stars scattered like twinkling diamonds against the inky backdrop. The absence of the moon's light casts deep shadows, giving a mysterious aura to the square.

The well-tended garden in the centre of the square appears as a silhouette, its flowers and shrubs shrouded in shadow. The absence of the moon's gentle illumination lends an air of uncertainty to the fountain, its splashing waters sounding eerily louder in the stillness.

Despite the darkness, you can still perceive a faint glimmer of light on the horizon, signalling the imminent arrival of dawn. The first rays of sunlight break through the horizon, casting a warm, golden glow on the edges of the square, gradually dispelling the darkness.

Regardless of the anxiety I feel, I stand tall. As daybreak approaches, the town square slowly comes to life. The first early risers emerge from their homes, carrying bags and sipping cups of steaming coffee from the nearby cafes. The anticipation that hung in the air dissipates, replaced by a renewed sense of normalcy. No one appears to notice me at first, lost in their own daily routines and thoughts. I remain in my spot and a gentle breeze sweeps through the town square, causing the bottom of your dress to sway softly in its embrace.

A woman carrying a wicker basket full of what looks like the day's washings must have noticed the movement from the corner of her eyes, because when she looks up and sees me, she drops the basket and screams. The rest of the villagers take notice, and they all stop what they are doing to stare at me. The woman takes off, back to the way I had first come from. The sudden stillness in the square intensifies as the villagers continue to stare, their collective gaze following the woman's departure. Whispers and murmurs start to circulate, and there is a palpable tension in the air.

Almost as quickly as the woman left, she is back. A large man trails behind her, his face stormy and his gait determined.

This must be the leader, I think to myself.

"Fae," he spits out venomously, and crosses his arms.

"You better have the information we want," he finishes.

I brace myself against this man's negative energy. I was expecting dislike, but this man radiated hatred. As the townspeople formed a tight circle around us, their eyes filled with anticipation and curiosity. Whispers and hushed conversations rippled through the crowd, eager to witness the impending exchange between the two of us. The air was thick with tension.

"The moon has been missing from the sky for too long," I begin.

"The moon has been missing from the sky for too

long," my voice resonated through the quietude, carrying a hint of longing. "Its radiant glow, once a steadfast companion, has vanished, leaving us in darkness. Its absence has left a void, not just in the celestial canvas above, but within our hearts and souls as well. The moon, with its gentle light, has been a beacon of hope and tranquillity. Its phases marked the passage of time, guiding us through both joyous and sombre moments. It inspired poets, ignited lovers' passions, and whispered secrets to those who sought solace under its luminescence."

A murmur of agreement and nostalgia quietly reverberated through the crowd, echoing the sentiment I had expressed.

"But in its absence, we have also been gifted an opportunity," I continue, my voice carrying a note of optimism. "An opportunity to do the right thing. The powers of the Fae are intrinsic to our being, bestowed upon us from the moment of our birth, and cannot be transferred or shared. But we can share our accumulated knowledge and skills, and perhaps you could do the same. We do not need to hate one another for our differences, but embrace and celebrate them. Our differences make us unique and interesting as individuals and as a society. Instead of fostering hatred and division, we should strive to cultivate understanding, empathy, and respect for one another."

As I speak, I notice that most of the townspeople are almost imperceptibly nodding their heads in agreement with my words. But their leader's breath is deepening and quickening, while his face is reddening in anger.

"And when the moon finally returns," I conclude, my voice filled with a sense of hope, "we will celebrate its radiant presence like never before. We will gather beneath its glow, rejoicing in the reunion with our celestial friend, knowing that our shared efforts brought back the luminosity that once adorned our nights."

CALIDA

$\mathcal{I}$ try to make eye contact with each person surrounding me, hoping that my words have been enough to convince them of the moon's safe return. As I make eye contact with each villager, I can see a range of emotions reflecting in their expressions —curiosity, uncertainty, and perhaps a glimmer of hope. But before I can speak again, the man clears his throat. The attention of the square turns toward him, waiting in anticipation.

"You–" He sputters angrily.

"You demon! You are a silver-tongued liar. If you do not meet the demands by this evening, you will never see the moon again! Consequences be damned!" His hair, that had started out coiffed, is now dishevelled and sweaty strands stick to his forehead and neck.

He glares at the once sympathetic townspeople, daring them to defy his wishes. An untamed fire flickers within his gaze, and I instinctively step back. The crowd parts to let me move, as if they know what will happen next. For the first time since I arrived at the village square, I am frightened.

This man won't hurt me, will he? I am not so certain.

He inches towards me, and the air seems to thicken. Each step he takes appears to amplify his presence, as if he is growing in size before my eyes. The shifting dynamics between myself and the man intensify, heightening the anticipation and uncertainty that lingers in the air.

His figure looms larger, casting a shadow that stretches across the ground. The wildfire in his eyes flickers with an intensity that mirrors the building tension between us. The proximity between us both feels charged with an unspoken confrontation, and the energy that radiates from him is almost tangible.

I do not see who it is, but a voice in the crowd whispers one word I cannot ignore - "run."

Feeling a surge of instinctual fear and urgency, I gather the flowing fabric of my dress and, without hesitation; I break into a sprint. The primal instinct for self-preservation takes over as my heart pounds in my chest, propelling me forward with all my might. Each step I take carries me farther away from the encroaching presence of the man, as if my very life depends on it.

The villagers, momentarily startled by my sudden movement, watch in astonishment as I flee with a desperate determination. Their initial anticipation gives way to confusion and concern, their gazes following my rapid escape. Whispers ripple through the crowd, mingling with the sound of my hurried footsteps.

As I weave through the maze-like streets, my surroundings unfocus in a blur of motion. My senses heighten, attuned to every sound and movement behind me, driving me to push your physical limits. The fear that propelled me into this flight intensifies, and I can't shake the feeling that there is genuine danger lurking in the man's presence.

With each passing moment, I strive to put more distance between myself and the perceived threat. The world becomes a smudge as I navigate the winding paths, my focus honed on my escape. The bustling village seems to fade into the background as my desperate flight takes precedence.

The rhythm of my footsteps pounds in my ears, driving me onward, my lungs burning with exertion. The fear that propelled me forward acts as both a catalyst and a burden, urging me to go further, faster.

I reach the edge of town and have no intention of stopping until I reach my sisters. But the sound of crying snaps me out of my focused sprint. It pierces through the rush of wind and the pounding of my own footsteps, drawing my attention to its source. The sound of crying tugs at my heart, momentarily pulling me out of my desperate escape.

I skid to a halt, my breath ragged, and turn my gaze towards the direction from which the cries emanate.

The cottage I had passed on my way into the village catches my attention once again, and I cautiously creep forward. On the south side of the quaint home, a window is cracked, and against my better judgement, I peer in. The room is dimly lit, with a solitary candle casting flickering shadows on the worn wooden furniture. The air carries a musty scent, as if the room has been sealed for some time. Despite the crack in the window, the atmosphere inside feels stagnant, adding to the sense of mystery that envelopes the space.

Upon closer inspection, I notice an assortment of curious objects scattered across a worn table. A weathered journal lies open, its pages filled with handwritten notes and sketches. Parchment maps, faded and delicate, are pinned to the wall, depicting unfamiliar lands and intricate paths.

As my gaze wanders further, it settles upon a young girl. She is curled in a tight ball on the wooden floor, her body wracked with sobs. As the candlelight flickers, I can see her face - it's the young girl that offered me comfort by the pond.

"I've ruined everything", the girl moans repeatedly.

As I watch her, my heart swells with empathy, recognizing that the magnitude of her worries is not always proportional to her physical stature. In this moment, I am reminded that every individual carries a unique story, their worries often concealed beneath the surface, unseen by casual observers.

As my attention remains fixated on the young girl, my senses unaware of the approaching presence, a sudden shift in the atmosphere sends a shiver down my spine. A lingering silence hangs in the air, disrupted only by the sound of my own breathing. It is then, with a jolt of realisation, that I notice someone standing behind me.

Slowly, I turn, my heart pounding with a mixture of surprise and apprehension. My eyes meet the gaze of the man from the town, whose presence looms with an intensity that cannot be ignored.

"You've made a grave error," the man says with a sickening grin.

CALIDA

In the room I was just observing through the window, I find myself bound by chains at the foot of the bed. I scan my surroundings, my gaze darting in every direction, as I desperately seek to orient myself and understand my current situation. A jolt of realisation courses through me as I feel the cold, unyielding touch of the iron chains against my skin. The clinking sound echoes in the room, a stark reminder that these restraints are impervious to Fae magic.

Surprised by a sudden cough, my attention snaps to the young girl, who huddles in the corner of the small room, visibly trembling with fear. My instincts kick in, and I shift into a defensive stance. My senses heightened as I scan the room, searching for any sign of a potential threat or danger.

She's afraid of me, I realise after a moment.

I raise my hands slightly with my palms facing her, doing my best to show the girl I am not a threat. Her shaking lessens, and she regards me curiously. I keep quiet, letting the young girl study me.

"You are the Fae in charge of the moon," she mumbles.

My eyes widen in surprise, and I speak without thinking.

"How on earth would you know such a thing?" I blurt out, and the girl quickly shies away from my outburst.

Drat, I chastise myself. Proceed with caution. I give myself a warning before attempting to regain the small bit of trust I had with the girl.

"I am Calida," I begin. "And you are correct. I am the Fae in charge of raising and lowering the moon."

The girl is silent, her large brown eyes watching me warily. I try to give her a small smile and maintain a gentle, reassuring tone in my voice as I speak to her. Understanding the importance of building trust, I choose my words carefully, attempting to convey my intentions.I remain patient, giving her the space and time she needs to process and respond, ready to adjust my approach accordingly.

"Do you know the man that has trapped me here?" I ask.

She nods and gets a faraway look in her eyes. Biting her lower lip, I can tell that the girl is fighting back tears, and I remain quiet.

"He's my father," the girl explains. "Well, my adopted

father. I made a decision he wasn't happy with, and unless I change my mind, I am trapped in my room with you."

As the girl opens up, sharing her story, my heart goes out to her. I listen intently, acknowledging the complex dynamics she faces with her adopted father. Sensing her vulnerability, I respond with empathy and compassion.

"I'm here to support you, and I understand that sometimes difficult decisions can strain relationships," I say, my voice filled with understanding. "Remember that you have the right to make choices that feel true to yourself."

The girl's response catches me off guard as she breaks down in tears.

"I am the reason for all of this mess!"

The girl's face reflects a palpable sense of guilt, visible in her expression and body language.

She is clearly confused; I decide.

"Your adoptive father has done this misdeed, not you," I try to reassure her. But the girl shakes her head and sobs harder.

"I stole the moon," she admits, and it leaves us both momentarily stunned by the magnitude of her words. The admission hangs in the air, heavy with both the weight of guilt and the intrigue of the extraordinary act she has just revealed.

"You–" I start. "What–" I try to speak but keep stuttering. "How?" I ask, and my heart feels like it's going to beat right out of my chest.

As the girl explains, a flood of questions swirls in my mind. However, recognizing the importance of allowing her to share her story uninterrupted, I attempt to quiet my curiosity. I focus on being present, giving her my undivided attention, and listening attentively to every detail she discloses.

As she finishes her story, she finally introduces herself.

"I'm Erissa," she mumbles, looking down at the floor. "I am so sorry for what I did."

As I gaze into the young girl's eyes, the sincerity of her remorse is unmistakable. It radiates from her expression, tugging at my heartstrings. In that moment, a profound sense of empathy washes over me, over-riding any lingering anger or resentment. I find myself unable to resist the overwhelming urge to extend forgiveness, understanding that we all make mistakes and deserve a chance for redemption.

"How can I make this right?" Erissa looks at me for guidance.

I sigh, thinking hard.

"By now my sisters will know I am missing," I muse. "Most likely, they will send a few of our best fliers to comb the area subtly in hopes I am easily found."

As Erissa shares her insight on her father, my focus intensifies. The urgency of the situation becomes clear as she reveals her father is likely mobilising the towns-people, rallying support for his plan with the moon. Understanding the potential repercussions, I nod in understanding and contemplate our next course of action.

"We need to act swiftly then," I say, a sense of determination in my voice. "We must communicate our intentions and seek understanding from the villagers. Together, we can present an alternative perspective, appealing to their sense of reason and empathy."

She nods. "How? You are shackled, and I am not strong enough to break you free. Not to mention the villagers do not care for me, as my parentage is unknown. Though unlikely, I could have Fae lineage," she admits.

"That occurred to me after you told me your history," I admit. "But when I spoke to the villagers earlier, I could see compassion in them. My words moved them, despite my being a Fae. I think I could sway them," I finish with conviction.

"As for escaping these chains," I give Erissa a loaded look. "Do not be afraid," I say cryptically before I transform.

As my arms elongate into wings, I can feel the shackles loosening. I look at Erissa and her mouth is agape, but I see recognition in her eyes. I don't need to complete my transformation this time, as my wrists were the only parts of me that were bound. My bones click and shift once again, and the feathers that once adorned my body dissolve, revealing smooth, pale skin underneath.

"You–You're the swan that was crying by the pond!" Erissa shouts.

I nod and walk towards her. "You showed great kindness to me that day, and the memory of your compassion lingers within me still. It was a defining moment in my life, where your selflessness touched my heart and left a mark on my soul. The way you extended your hand, without hesitation or judgement, reminded me of the inherent goodness that exists in this world."

ERISSA

 $\mathcal{E}$ rissa cries at the kindness Calida has shown her. She has made some horrible mistakes, but at that moment, she feels a glimmer of hope and redemption. The weight of her past actions bears heavily on her shoulders, but Calida's unwavering kindness breaks through the walls of self-condemnation that have enveloped her. The tears that stream down Erissa's cheeks carry with them a mixture of remorse, relief, and gratitude. She realises that although she has made mistakes; they do not solely define her. There is room for growth, forgiveness, and the opportunity to make amends. With a newfound determination, Erissa vows to learn from her past and channel her experiences into creating a better future.

"I have an idea on how to get out," Erissa speaks. "If you transform back into a swan, I think you'll be just small enough to squeeze out of the cracked window."

Calida nods at Erissa and begins her transformation. Erissa watches again with awe, as Calida's form shifts, her human features gradually giving way to the graceful swan. As her body undergoes its magnificent metamorphosis, her shape and size shrink, adapting to the elegant proportions of a swan. Feathers begin to sprout and spread across her body, forming a splendid plumage of iridescent white. The once-human eyes now gleam with a deep, ancient wisdom, reflecting the spirit of a creature born to soar. She nods to me and hops from the floor to the bed, and the bed to the nightstand.

With a graceful arch of her webbed feet and a gentle flutter of her wings, Calida positions herself on the windowsill, readying herself for the daring escape. I can feel the air crackle with anticipation as her gaze meets mine, a silent reassurance passing between us. And then, with a surge of courage and determination, Calida propels herself into the open air. Erissa waits with bated breath, and moments later Calida unlocks her bedroom door.

With a warm smile, Calida extends her hand toward Erissa, a silent gesture of support and camaraderie. Erissa, filled with a mixture of anticipation and resolve, takes her hand lightly, their fingers intertwining in a bond of trust and determination. Together, they walk toward the front door, their steps synchronised, hearts aligned in a shared purpose.

As they step outside, the evening sun begins its descent, casting a warm golden glow over the horizon.

The sky slowly transforms, transitioning from vibrant hues of orange and pink to deepening shades of purple and blue. The fading light paints a canvas of tranquillity, creating an atmosphere of peacefulness as darkness approaches.

Erissa and Calida take a moment to admire the changing colours, their gazes lingering on the fading sunlight that bathes the world in its final caress. Erissa finds solace in the twilight's quietude, a respite from the tumultuous events of the day. In this serene moment, she gathers her thoughts, reflecting on the journey that awaits them under the veil of nightfall.

With renewed purpose, they continue their path, guided by the dimming light and the steady beat of their hearts. As they walk back to the town centre, they are interrupted by a sparrow that quickly metamorphosed into a beautiful dark-skinned woman.

"Calida!" the Fae yelled. "Are you alright?"

Calida nods and embraces the woman. "I am safe, Nettelia. But we must hurry if we want to retrieve the moon, lest we lose it forever," Calida responds. "This is Erissa, the adoptive daughter of the man whose destiny now intertwines with their own."

There is a flicker of an unfamiliar expression on Nettelia's face, one that puzzles Erissa, leaving her curious yet unable to decipher its meaning. It passes fleetingly, almost as if it was never there, leaving Erissa with a sense of intrigue and a lingering question in her mind. For now, however, Erissa must focus on the pressing matters at hand, letting the brief glimpse of an unknown expression serve as a reminder that there is much yet to be discovered in this intricate tapestry of intertwined destinies. With determination, she sets her sights forward, ready to face the challenges that lie ahead, while keeping Nettelia's hidden depths in the back of her mind, awaiting when the puzzle pieces will reveal themselves.

"I will gather the others," Nettelia announces. "We will be ready for whatever you need from us." With that, she becomes her sparrow-self, and she pushes off the ground, soaring into the open sky.

With night approaching fast, Erissa and Calida run to the town square.

"My father does not make idle threats," Erissa huffed, her breathing shallow. "If he said he will destroy the moon if he does not get what he wants, he is serious."

The thought of her father's destructive intentions towards the moon sends a chill down Erissa's spine. The moon, a celestial symbol of beauty, mystery, and balance, holds a special place in her heart. She knows that if her father carries out his threat, it would unleash untold consequences upon the world, disrupting the delicate harmony of nature and plunging everything into chaos.

Erissa and Calida quicken their pace, their footsteps becoming more determined as they make their way through the dense forest. The familiar sights and sounds of nature slowly give way to signs of civilization. The towering trees gradually thin out, making room for the outskirts of the town to emerge. As they progress, the forest's green hues blend with the muted tones of buildings and the distant hum of activity. The scent of earthy moss and damp leaves mingles with the faint aroma of smoke and the buzz of distant conversations. The transition from the serenity of the woods to the bustling atmosphere of the town is gradual yet distinct.

Erissa's heart pounds in her chest, a mix of anticipation and apprehension coursing through her veins. The forest provided a sense of refuge and familiarity, but now, in the town's embrace, she faces the reality of the challenges that await her. The weight of her decisions and the imminent confrontation with her father press upon her shoulders, urging her onward.

With each step, the forest's tranquillity dissipates further, replaced by the vibrant energy of the town. The sight of people going about their daily lives, the market stalls brimming with goods, and the quaint architecture of familiar buildings greet them, beckoning them forward.

The two ladies exchange determined glances, silently reaffirming their commitment to their shared mission. They weave through the streets, navigating the labyrinthine paths and crowded alleys, fueled by a sense of purpose that propels them closer to their ultimate destination.

Erissa's heart skips a beat as she catches sight of her father standing tall and resolute in the centre of the bustling square. The familiar figure cuts a commanding presence, his stern expression etched with determination. He stands next to the grand water fountain, its cascading streams providing an ironic contrast to the tension that fills the air.

The square, usually a vibrant hub of community gatherings and cheerful conversations, is now filled with an undercurrent of anticipation and unease. Villagers gather around, their expressions ranging from curiosity to concern, as they take in the sight of Erissa's father, their leader, prepared to address them.

Erissa's gaze locks onto her father, her emotions swirling within her. There is a mixture of fear and longing, of anger and a desperate desire for reconciliation. She knows that this pivotal moment will shape the course of their relationship and perhaps even the destiny of the moon itself.

The large water fountain, a symbol of unity and abundance, stands as a silent witness to the impending confrontation. Its crystal-clear waters reflect the faces of the onlookers, mirroring the anticipation and uncertainty that permeates the atmosphere. It becomes a poignant backdrop, a visual representation of the choices that lie ahead. Erissa takes a deep breath, steadying herself as she prepares to confront her father and the weight of his demands.

ERISSA

s Erissa approaches the square and her father's imposing figure, she braces herself for the confrontation that awaits, ready to face the consequences of her decisions and to make a stand for what she believes in. The stage is set, and the outcome remains uncertain, but Erissa is resolved to do whatever it takes to right her wrongs.

Erissa's father catches sight of her standing in the square, a mixture of surprise and anger washes over his face. The lines on his forehead deepen, and his scowl becomes more pronounced, a visible reflection of his displeasure. His eyes lock onto Erissa, and a tense silence hangs in the air.

The weight of disappointment is palpable as Erissa's father realises that she has defied his orders and ventured out of the room where she was confined. The intensity of his scowl communicates his disapproval and the gravity of the situation. Erissa braces herself for the inevitable confrontation, knowing that her actions will only exacerbate her father's already simmering anger.

Erissa's father's scowl breaks abruptly as his eyes land on Calida standing by Erissa's side. A surge of fury courses through him, transforming his previously contained anger into an almost tangible force. The tension in the square intensifies, as his pent-up frustration demands release. Unable to contain himself any longer, he erupts with a thunderous voice that cuts through the air. His words carry the weight of disappointment, betrayal, and unyielding authority. The gathered villagers flinch at the sheer force of his fury, their gazes fixed on the unfolding confrontation. Every syllable that escapes his lips drips with disdain, his tone laced with a bitter mix of disbelief and indignation.

He storms towards Calida, and before there is time to react, slaps her across the face. Calida's head spins from the force, and she is knocked back several paces.

"YOU WRETCH!" he spits at her. "You have magicked your way into my daughter's heart and I will not stand for it!"

He reaches his hand back again, winding up for another blow.

Calida's head spins from the force of the slap, disoriented and stunned by the sudden act of aggression. As she struggles to regain her balance, a primal scream pierces the air, emanating from Erissa. The piercing sound reverberates through the square, startling not only Erissa's father but also the villagers who have gathered around. The high-pitched scream cuts through the tension like a knife, freezing everyone in their tracks.

"If you are unwilling to see that everything this Fae has said rings true, then we are truly doomed!" Erissa shrieked to her father.

"Do you truly not understand the repercussions of a world no longer blessed by the moon?"

Erissa's words cut through the charged atmosphere, her voice filled with a mix of desperation, frustration, and disbelief. The raw emotion in her plea reverberates through the square, causing a collective pause among the onlookers.

Her words, delivered with an intensity that cannot be ignored, challenge her father's perspective and demand his understanding. The weight of her conviction hangs heavy in the air, casting a shadow of doubt on the villagers' previous convictions.

"Insolent child! You will treat me with reverence and respect - or you are no daughter of mine!" Erissa's father angrily repeats his sentiments.

"I never should have allowed your mother to take you in as a baby," he hisses. "You have always been ungrateful, and your blood is probably just as impure as this creature's."

He gestures wildly at Calida, and spits at her feet. Erissa turns to the villagers, hoping to convince them of the impending danger and the truth behind Calida's words. Erissa's voice quivers with a mix of urgency and determination as she addresses the crowd, her eyes searching for signs of understanding and empathy.

"Listen, my fellow villagers," Erissa begins, her voice projecting with a newfound strength. "We stand at the precipice of a catastrophic loss, a loss that goes beyond our comprehension. The moon, the celestial guardian that has watched over us for generations, is in grave peril."

She pauses, allowing her words to sink in, the weight of the moment hanging heavily in the air. The villagers, their attention now fully captured, lean in closer, their curiosity piqued by Erissa's impassioned plea.

"The moon's absence will unleash unimaginable consequences upon our world," Erissa continues, her voice trembling with a mix of fear and conviction. "Its gentle light guides us, nourishes the land, and shapes the ebb and flow of nature. Without it, darkness and chaos will descend upon us, disrupting the delicate balance we rely upon."

Erissa's gaze sweeps across the faces of the villagers, seeking a connection, a shared understanding of the magnitude of the situation. She implores them to set aside their doubts and embrace the truth that Calida has brought forth, even if it challenges their preconceived notions.

"I know you are no supporter of mine. My unknown heritage makes you nervous, and your lack of understanding leads you to fear what you don't know," Erissa addresses the villagers, her voice firm but tinged with a hint of sadness. "But I stand before you not as an outsider, but as one of your own. My love for this town, this land, and its people runs deep within me."

She pauses, allowing her words to sink in, her eyes scanning the crowd, searching for any flicker of empathy or understanding. Some villagers shift uncomfortably, their preconceived notions beginning to waver in the face of Erissa's sincerity.

"I may be different, but it is precisely because of our differences that we have the opportunity to learn from one another," Erissa continues, her voice steady. "We have the chance to break free from the shackles of fear and embrace the beauty of diversity, the richness that comes from acceptance and unity."

A murmur ripples through the crowd, the cogs of realisation turning within their minds. Erissa's words challenge their prejudices, urging them to open their hearts and minds to a broader perspective.

"I stand here not as a threat, but as someone who shares your hopes, dreams, and concerns," Erissa emphasises, her voice filled with conviction. "We all have a stake in the protection of our world, the preservation of the moon's blessing. It is a responsibility that falls upon every one of us, regardless of our backgrounds or origins."

She takes a step forward, bridging the distance between herself and the villagers, a gesture of vulnerability and solidarity. The tension in the air eases, replaced by a sense of curiosity and newfound empathy.

"I ask you, my fellow villagers, to look beyond the surface and see the shared humanity that connects us all," Erissa implores, her voice carrying a note of hope. "Together, we can overcome the barriers that divide us, unite our strengths, and safeguard the legacy of our town and the moon that graces our nights."

As the silence hangs in the air, the fate of the moon and their world hangs in the balance. It is a moment of decision, where the collective will of the villagers will shape the course of their shared destiny.

*H*er words hang in the air, resonating with those who dare to listen. The villagers, once sceptical and divided, now stand at a crossroads, contemplating the power of acceptance and the strength that can be found in unity. It is a crucial moment where the transformative seeds of understanding and compassion have the potential to bloom, forever changing the destiny of their community.

My gaze moves from face to face, taking in the range of expressions that reflect the inner turmoil within each individual. Some wear looks of skepticism, their brows furrowed in doubt, while others show signs of introspection, their eyes reflecting a glimmer of newfound understanding.

I resist the urge to interject, to share my own insights or offer reassurance. This moment belongs to Erissa, and it is her sincerity, her connection to the town and its people, that will pave the way for genuine acceptance and unity. My role, for now, is to observe and support from the sidelines. As the silence stretches, a flicker of change ripples through the crowd. Whispers of conversation rise, signalling the villagers' inner deliberations. I can sense the stirrings of transformation, the breaking down of barriers, and the potential for a shift in perspective.

It is a delicate dance, this act of letting them find their own way, their own truth. The path towards understanding and acceptance is one that must be taken willingly, without coercion or manipulation. So, I stand in patient vigilance, holding the space for their individual journeys to unfold.

I watch Erissa take a step forward, bridging the distance between herself and the villagers, a gesture of vulnerability and solidarity. The tension in the air eases, replaced by new found empathy.

Erissa's father stands amidst the crowd, his face a canvas of conflicting emotions. Anger and frustration battle against the growing empathy and understanding exhibited by some of the townspeople. As he witnesses the sympathetic reactions from those around him, his face reddens with a mix of embarrassment and indignation. His clenched fists and rigid posture betray his inner turmoil.

As Erissa's father extends his hand, a hush falls over the square. All eyes are drawn to a woman who steps forward, her movements deliberate and purposeful. My gaze locks onto the woman. She is shaking with anticipation. With one swift motion, the woman reaches into the folds of her cloak, her hand emerging clutching a small, shimmering orb. The orb glows with an ethereal radiance, casting a gentle luminosity on the faces of those gathered.

As the woman holds the orb aloft, the moon's reflection dances in my eyes, igniting a flicker of determination. The journey to reclaim what was lost, to heal the wounds inflicted upon their world, unfolds before them. With unwavering determination, I step forward, but Erissa's father is too quick.

Consumed by anger and resentment, he steps forward from the crowd. His eyes glint with a sinister determination as he fixates on the small, radiant orb held by the woman. Erissa's father's hands tremble with malice, driven by a desperate need to see the orb shattered, to obliterate any chance of restoring the moon's power and influence. His steps are purposeful and menacing as he approaches the woman and the precious artefact she safeguards. With each stride, his intent becomes clearer, his actions a stark contrast to the hope and determination that fills the air.

As he reaches out, his fingers curl into a fist, poised to strike. Hatred fuels his every movement, his desire to extinguish the light that represents everything he resents and fears. The orb, a symbol of unity and restoration, becomes a target for his destructive rage.

But in the face of this dark presence, there is resistance. The crowd gasps collectively, their collective will to protect the orb palpable. Defiance flickers in the eyes of those who have found solace and purpose in the pursuit of harmony. They step forward, a human barrier formed by their shared determination to shield the orb from harm. Erissa's father hesitates, momentarily shaken by the strength and unity of those who stand against him. The weight of their collective belief in the orb's significance strikes a chord within him, stirring fragments of doubt and conflict within his tormented soul. His face indicates that he is standing at a precipice, teetering on the edge of a decision that will not only shape his own fate but the destiny of the entire town.

The anger that once consumed him dissipates, evaporating into the air like a heavy fog lifting. The man's stance falters, his shoulders slumping and his body crumpling under the weight of his conflicting emotions. In a sudden and unexpected moment of vulnerability, his hardened facade crumbles.

As the tension seeps out of his being, a mix of regret, sorrow, and realisation fills the void left by his anger. The magnitude of his actions, fueled by misguided motives and a distorted perception, becomes painfully clear to him. The weight of the consequences, both personal and collective, settles upon his shoulders.

"What have I done?" He speaks harshly to himself.

He looks up at me, his eyes welling with tears. A profound transformation sweeps through him, as if the weight of his choices has finally caught up with his conscience. His eyes, once filled with venomous determination, now reflect a depth of remorse and understanding. The man becomes a living embodiment of the complexities of human nature, capable of both darkness and redemption.

In his crumpled state, he symbolises the fragility of pride and the profound impact of compassion and empathy. The transformative power of empathy reaches deep within him, unravelling the tangled knots of resentment and bitterness that had consumed his heart.

The town square is silent, and I turn to Erissa. Her face is unreadable, and for a moment I wonder if she is going to condemn her adoptive father for all the misdeeds he has done. But she steps towards him, wrapping her arms around his large torso.

"I forgive you," she whispers.

ERISSA

His arms wrap around her trembling form, enveloping her in a cocoon of warmth and love. The intensity of his embrace conveys a depth of longing, regret, and a desperate desire for reconciliation. The hug ends, and Erissa pulls back reluctantly. Words left unspoken hang heavy in the air, but in their silence, there is an unspoken agreement to forge a new path forward. It is a testament to the power of forgiveness, to the ability to heal and rebuild even the most shattered relationships.

Her father releases his hold on her, his hands gently pushing back his dishevelled hair into a semblance of order. As he completes the gesture, his hair now arranged in a more acceptable manner, he meets his daughter's gaze. In that fleeting moment, their eyes lock, and a spark of understanding passes between them. It is a shared recognition that they have both grown, that they are ready to embark on a new chapter of their relationship.

With a nod of silent affirmation, her father takes a step forward, ready to face the challenges that lie ahead with newfound humility and open-mindedness. Her father's gaze shifts from his daughter to Calida, a flicker of remorse and reverence illuminating his eyes. With a trembling hand, he reaches out to Erissa's mother and retrieves the small, shimmering orb. Holding it delicately, he extends his arm toward Calida, offering her the precious artefact.

Calida, her gaze meeting his, sees the vulnerability in his gesture.The weight of the decision rests upon her, as she contemplates whether to accept this fragile offering and its potential for redemption. She delicately takes the moon, nodding towards the man.

"Thank you," she says before beginning to leave the square. It was almost midnight, and the moon needed to be returned to its rightful place in the sky.

"Wait!" Erissa shouts after the Fae. "I know I have no right, and I understand if my advances are rejected. But can I come back with you? I want to help you with this last task and make things right once again." Erissa looks at Calida with a longing in her eyes, a desire to make amends and be a part of the journey that lies ahead.

With a gentle nod, Calida accepts Erissa's offer, an unspoken agreement passing between them. Erissa's heart swells with a mix of gratitude, relief, and a renewed sense of purpose. The crowd parts, allowing the two ladies to leave the village centre unhindered. As

Erissa and Calida walk back towards the Hemlock Wilds, Erissa's senses sharpen, attuned to the subtle movements and whispers of the natural world around them. She notices a shift in the atmosphere, an undercurrent of watchfulness.

An owl perches on a tree branch, its golden eyes following their every step. Squirrels pause mid-scramble, their tiny paws frozen momentarily as they study the duo's passage. Even the rustling of leaves seems to hold a certain significance, as if nature itself is attuned to their presence.

"My sisters are guiding us back," Calida smiles at the curious Erissa.

With each passing encounter, Erissa finds solace and encouragement in the wildlife's subtle companionship. The steady flutter of wings above her head, the rustle of underbrush, and the gentle sway of branches become a comforting chorus of support, whispering assurances she is not alone.

They pass the familiar tree, and Erissa watches Calida sigh with relief at being back in her domain. The melodic chirping of birds and the gentle babbling of a nearby brook create a harmonious symphony, a reminder that they are part of a larger, interconnected world.

"We must hurry now," Calida urges.

Breaking through the veil of gracefully swaying willow trees, Calida and Erissa step into the heart of the meadow. Calida's sisters had already cast the stars one by one into the expanse above. Each star twinkled with ethereal brilliance, adorning the velvety darkness like precious gems.

Erissa can't help but be captivated by the enchanting scene. The purity and harmony of nature embrace her, filling her heart with a profound sense of peace. She takes a hesitant step forward, feeling the softness of the grass beneath her feet, as if the meadow itself welcomes her presence.

With a deep breath, Erissa closes her eyes for a moment, allowing herself to be fully present in this oasis of tranquillity. The meadow's energy courses through her, and to her great surprise, her skin glows a brilliant white. A gentle transformation unfolds, soft feathers sprouting from her skin, and her limbs elongating gracefully. A sense of lightness filled her being, as if the weight of the world had been lifted from her shoulders.

She had transformed into a beautiful dove, her wings adorned with delicate patterns of iridescent plumage.

"I believe your lineage is no longer in question, sister." Calida smiles widely.

"Will you do the honours?" Calida places the moon softly at Erissa's feet and watches as her talons pluck the delicate sphere from its resting place.

With a nod, Erissa unfurls her wings, showcasing a stunning display of shimmering hues of ivory and pearl. With a powerful beat of her wings, Erissa lifts herself off the ground, soaring higher and higher into the night sky. The world below shrinks in perspective as she ascends, leaving behind the burdens and limitations of her past. As she glides through the heavens, she raises the moon to its rightful place.

As Erissa glances downward, she looks at Calida; her face beaming with a mixture of joy and awe. She knows that this moment, this shared experience in the embrace of nature's splendour, is a gift. It ignites their spirits, reminding them of the significance of their journey and the power they hold within themselves.

AFTERWORD

Thank you for buying my book! I really hope you enjoy it. The continued support, by purchasing my books, helps support me so I can continue writing for my readers. Feel free to loan this out to other readers, I just ask that they *please* buy a copy if they like it. This helps tell my publisher how many people are reading my book, and of course it helps me write more books.

Thanks again! If I'm ever in your area signing books, please stop by and say hello! I'd love to meet you.

Enjoy the book, and don't forget to leave a review!